D0349228

Fionn Mac Cumhail's
Amazing Stories

Eddie Lenihan

Illustrated by Alan Clarke

MERCIER PRESS

Cork

www.mercierpress.ie

© Text: Eddie Lenihan, 2015

Stories adapted from *Irish Tales of Mystery and Magic,*
published by Mercier Press in 2006.

© Illustrations: Alan Clarke

Produced for Mercier Press by Teapot Press Ltd

Abridged and edited by Fiona Biggs
Designed by Alyssa Peacock & Tony Potter

ISBN: 978-1-78117-359-6

10 9 8 7 6 5 4 3 2 1

A CIP record for this title is available from the British Library

Printed and bound in China

CONTENTS

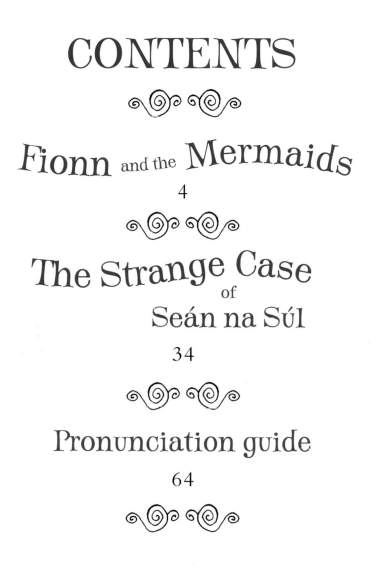

Fionn and the Mermaids

Fionn decides to go
fishing for young
Oisín's supper, but he
gets more than he
bargained for when
he finds himself in
the realm of the
mermaids battling
with ferocious sharks.

When Fionn's son, Oisín, was in his cradle he was so huge that Fionn and his wife had their hands full trying to feed him. He drank a barrel of milk every day, as much as their cows could produce, and left nothing for Fionn to drink with his dinner. Then the milk began to fail and Fionn decided to call a halt.

'That fellow will break us!' Fionn said. 'There's only one thing for it: we'll have to get him off the milk and on to some cheaper food.

'D'you know,' he said, 'the last time I was in Eamhain Macha I heard a rumour that fish is grand food for old people 'cos 'tis easy on the stomach. And if 'tis easy on old people, surely 'twould be just as good for a young lad! I'll go down to the sea tomorrow and see can I catch anything.'

That evening he went into the wood, cut a straight stick and brought it home. He reached into the thatch and pulled out the ball of catgut

he kept there for emergencies. He still needed
a hook, but he knew the very place where such
an item was to be got.

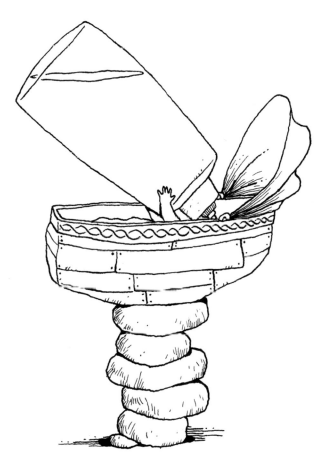

Next morning he crept to Oisín's cradle,
removed the wolf's tooth that tied his napkin,
then attached it to the end of his line and tiptoed
out of the house.

The sun was shining as Fionn strode on his way.
Suddenly, as if out of thin air, a dark figure bent
over a blackthorn stick appeared before him.

'Who are you?' he breathed.

Fionn Mac Cumhail, you are going this day to
the Black Cliff,' she wheezed. 'You're right, too.
That's the place you'll catch the fish. Take my word
for it,' she nodded, 'what you want is shark-meat.
But the problem is to catch them. They're a small
bit on the wicked side. But, sure, no bother
to a big fellow like yourself,' she smiled toothlessly.

'Go to the black pool under the cliff,' she
went on. 'Throw in your hook there and you'll
catch something.' She turned from him to take
something from a small black bag strung about her
neck. 'Put that on your hook and I'll guarantee
you won't come home empty-handed this day.'

Then she was off on her way, muttering to
herself among the trees.

Fionn hurried on, and he soon found himself
at the top of a cliff, looking down.

'*Hanam 'on diabhal,* isn't that the evil-looking
place, down there,' he whispered, gazing at the
stretch of water at the foot of the cliff. He could
see no trace of the bottom of the ocean through
its dark surface.

'I'd want to keep well back from the edge of this place,' he thought, measuring the cliff edge carefully. Then he gripped his rod, freed the hook, put his hand into his pouch and took out the thing the old woman had given him. He unwrapped it carefully, and there in his hand was a type of snail, two black eyes looking up at him from the ends of little horns on top of its head. Its body was green, with yellow spots, and Fionn felt his skin beginning to crawl.

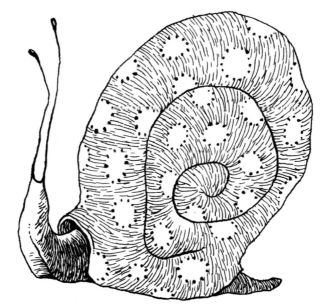

'He's the quarest divil I ever saw,' he thought
to himself, not knowing whether to stick the hook
in it or not. In the end he did, good and tight, too,
but as soon as its point met the snail Fionn's ears
were pierced by a painful 'SqueEEEE!!'

Fionn dropped his line, with the creature
struggling at the end of it, over the edge of the cliff.
Down it went, and plop! into the dark water.

He expected the rod to be dragged out of
his hands, so he braced himself, left leg to the front,
rod over knee, waiting. Nothing. He shuffled,
changed his position. Still nothing. He began to
feel bored.

After a few minutes of this Fionn growled,
'Ah, to hell with it! I'll have a smoke,' and put
the rod under his foot. Suddenly, without warning,
there was a vicious tug on the line and the rod was
almost pulled from under his boot.

'*Hanam 'on diabhal*, what's here?' he gabbled, dropping his pipe and snatching at the rod. Down, down it went, and Fionn pulled and strained to hold it, but the more he held it back the stronger the pull became. He was dragged nearer and nearer to the edge of the cliff. He dug in his heels, but he could get no grip on the bare rock.

'What'll I do?' he gibbered. 'If I let go, my rod is gone for ever. I'd better hang on, whatever happens.'

Just then the rod jerked and he was pulled over the edge of the cliff. Down, down into the water he plunged, holding on to the rod for dear life.

The rod and his hands were yanked out, full stretch, before him, and he was off through the water like a fish. He strained, wriggled and began to turn blue, and then the creature that was pulling the rod swerved into a dark opening in the seabed. Before Fionn knew anything he was gasping for breath and splashing madly in a large underwater cave.

On one side of the cave there were three big
pillars, bright lamps hanging from chains down
between them, and on the other were three steps
leading up out of the water. Fionn found himself
eye-to-eye with a strange-looking creature.

The creature began to cut with angry strokes at
its fish-like tail. Fionn saw the long scaly tail and
half-body, the woman's face, hands and hair, and
he remembered a story he had heard in his youth, a
tale of mermaids under the sea.

He felt a sudden tug on his line as the mermaid
flung something from her, and he realised that he
had hooked her tail and only now had she freed
herself! If looks could kill, Fionn would have died
at that moment.

'Who are you?' she asked, crossly. 'What evil
chance brought you to this place?'

'Look, I was only trying to get a bit of fish
for the young lad at home,' he tried to explain.

'Hmmm,' she said, 'I don't know whether to believe you or not. But I'm going to take you to meet our queen, and she'll make no mistakes. Follow me.'

Fionn climbed up the three steps and trudged after her, boots squelching. They went left, right, then left again, round and round, and Fionn knew he had little hope of finding his way back. Then, suddenly, they were in a long, bright hall, with the mermaid queen sitting on a glittering throne at one end. Around her were three of the most evil-looking fish that Fionn had ever seen, smirking at him with their huge yellow teeth showing.

Fionn approached the throne. The queen glared at him from a height.

'Explain yourself!' she shouted at him.

'I was only trying to catch a few sharks for my hungry lad at home,' faltered Fionn.

The word 'sharks' was no sooner out of his mouth when he knew that he had said the wrong thing, for the three monsters behind the throne set up a gnashing and rattling of their teeth that almost deafened him. He cringed.

'All right. Look!' he said, reasonably. 'If you let me out of here now I'll go peacefully on my way. There'd be less risk hunting rabbits than in this fishing thing, anyway, bad luck to it. A fellow'd be better off racing his shadow up and down a hill than standing up on a cliff waiting for the legs to be swept from under him.'

'Racing ...' said she. 'Are you interested in racing? That's it so. A race is what we'll have.'

'What kind of race had you in your head?' asked Fionn, wondering at the strange turn things were taking.

'You know the steps where you came up
out of the water?' she said.

'I do,' said Fionn.

'You know the cliff you fell down over?
Well, between those two is the race-course.'
She smiled coldly.

'Go down those steps again, into the water and
start swimming for the cliff. You'll get ten minutes
of a start on my friends here' – turning to smile at
the sharks – 'and if you can get to the cliff and
climb it before they catch you, well and good.'

'And if I can't?' shouted Fiann.

'Well and bad!' she answered icily. She clapped
her hands. At once Fionn's mermaid returned,
bringing a little glass container filled with water.
'When I take away my finger from this little hole,'
she said, 'the water will drip out. In ten minutes
it will be empty. I hope you're well on your way
by then.'

The eyes of the three sharks
behind the throne were glued to
the little jar, with occasional glances
at Fionn, as a person might check
a joint of meat cooking.

'Ah, here! I'll do it,' Fionn rasped,
thundering down the hallway.
Running blindly, by some miracle
he found himself at the three steps.
He leaped from the top step, his
fishing rod in his right hand,
and struggled downwards to
the mouth of the cave. He
pushed the rod under his belt
and fixed his mind's eye on
the cliff face.

He broke for the surface but had only gone a
little way when he heard, one after another,
three splashes behind him.

Seconds later the three evil-looking beasts were
swimming around him, eyes glaring coldly.

Snatching his rod from his belt, Fionn guided
it straight into the biggest shark's eye, and the eye
was out! The shark groped his way back home,
beaten.

The second shark glided up behind Fionn, intent
on snapping off his legs, but in an instant Fionn
had whipped off his long boot and pushed it over
the fierce nose and mouth.

The shark's tail flapped wildly as the terrible
smelly contents of the boot did their evil work,
then the shark shuddered and sank slowly to the
sea floor.

But now Fionn's way was barred by the fangs of the last shark. It opened its mouth and showed every tooth in a huge snarl.

Fionn opened his own mouth in an even more horrible leer, on account of his having only four stumpy black teeth. The shark paused in shock, and Fionn groped under its jaw and began to tickle.

As the cruel mouth closed in a smile, Fionn's other fist hit the shark like a hammer and splinters of teeth were soon spreading to the four corners of the ocean floor.

Fionn rushed for the cliff face, climbed it and sat panting feverishly on top.

Then he hurried back home.

He had travelled most of the way, when before him he saw a dark bent figure.

''Tis ... 'tis early you're back,' the old woman stuttered, hiding something inside her shawl.

'And no thanks to you, either,' snarled Fionn.

'What did I see you hiding there under that shawl? Come on! Out with it!'

'That's nothing to do with you,' she squealed.

'We'll see about that,' he grated, catching her hand, exposing a leather money bag.

'O, you bad thing, you! You evil oul' *cailleach*!' he roared. It was the money bag that he kept in the little hole near the fireplace at home. Snatching the bag in his left hand, his right hand tightened around her neck, and he lifted her up and flung her into the air. Off she streaked through the sky like a shooting star or some misguided missile, and was never seen in those parts again.

Fionn ran for home.

He screeched to a halt at the door and fell into the house, only to be met by his wife.

'Well? Did you bring it?' she asked.

'Oh, yes. I got it back safe an' sound.' There was pride in his voice.

'What are you talking about?' said she.

'Our money,' he smiled toothlessly.

She looked at the bag. 'That isn't our money bag at all,' she said. She went to the fireplace and pulled out Fionn's money bag.

'Crom be good to me,' he groaned, 'but I attacked her in the wrong!'

'Never mind that,' said his wife. 'How are you going to feed the child?'

'Well,' said Fionn, 'I suppose I could buy some good milk cows with all this gold.'

And off he went to the fair, bought six black cows and carried them home, three under each arm. And from that day on there was peace in the house and Oisín grew up handsome, good-natured and wise, all because of the milk of those six good cows and Fionn's journey to the realm of the mermaids.

The Strange Case
of
Seán na Súl

Fionn and St Patrick are sent for when a strange man without eyes bewitches people and makes them disappear. When they go to the rescue, they uncover a strange story.

One day Fionn Mac Cumhail and St Patrick were having a meeting when a messenger arrived, together with fifty men of the Fianna, and their hunting dogs, including Bran and Sceolan.

The messenger handed a letter to Patrick, whose face went white when he read it. 'Fionn,' he said, 'we must be off at once. I can't tell you why until we cross the Shannon, but we have to leave now!'

They set out and marched without stopping until they saw the big river. One of the Fianna, Diarmaid, organised boats for their crossing, and they all set sail. As soon they were across, Patrick gathered everyone around him and read from the letter:

'Patrick, you holy man! Get Fionn Mac Cumhail and whatever men you can, and hurry to help us quick, or there won't be anyone left to tell the world about the terrible things that are happening in *Tuath Clae*.'

'Well, what are we waiting here for?' barked Fionn. 'Come on! Every minute counts, by the sound of it.'

They went north, pounding the roads. When
they came near to Liscannor they noticed that there
was an eerie silence over all the countryside. Not a
soul was to be seen.

They were crossing the river near Ballyvaughan
when Patrick spotted, on the far bank, a withered
old man with straggly white hair, his chin resting on
his hands and his hands resting on a stick.

They were halfway across the river when they
heard the old man shout, 'God save you! Where are
you going in this cursed place?'

Patrick explained their errand. As soon as the old
man heard their names his eyes brightened and he
whispered, 'My prayers are answered. You came!'

'What's happening in this country?' Fionn asked.
'Where are all the people?'

'They're all stolen away,' said the old man sadly,
'to *Tír na nÓg* or some place like that, I'm not sure.
This day three weeks ago a strange-looking man
with a bandaged face came to our country with a

box under each arm. The people gathered to watch him wherever he'd go and as soon as he had their attention he'd put his hand to the bandage and wind it off slowly. And when it came to where his eyes should be there were no eyes in his face, none at all. Of course, the first question the people would ask was, "What happened your eyes, poor man?"

'At that he'd open one of the boxes – and there were his eyes inside! And when those eyes looked at the people they froze to the spot. Then he touched each one of them with a small black stick and they shrank down to the size of *ciaróg*s, and then he put them all into the other box. Seán na Súl they call him and he has the place emptied.'

'Where is he now?' asked Fionn.

'They say he is in Aughnanure. Every day he carries off a box full of people from there. And they'll never again be seen unless you can do something. I'd be gone myself too, only I was sick in bed when he came, so I wasn't able to get a look at his eyes. Don't leave me here, the last of all my people in an empty land.'

'We'll help all we can,' Fionn said, 'but how can we avoid being caught ourselves?'

'You have to get the two boxes away from him. Because if you capture the box with his eyes in it he won't be able to see any more.'

Fionn, Patrick and the Fianna set off, marching northwards, then west, until they got to the small hill at Aughnanure.

Crouching low, they climbed the little hill until they reached the summit and could see the fort perched on another low hill just ahead of them.

'Look at the gate!' hissed Diarmuid, and all eyes peered at the open gates of the fort, where a large bulky figure sat cross-legged, his head completely wrapped in a bandage and each of his hands resting heavily on a box, one on each side of him.

Suddenly, two men came into view. Immediately one of the boxes, the one under his right arm, snapped open and a pair of glittering eyes lay there, glaring out. The men were frozen to the spot and Seán na Súl reached into a pocket. He drew out a short black stick, touched each man and like a flash they shrank to the size of mice. With a low, evil cackle he gathered them up and swept them into the other box.

'That's our man,' whispered Fionn. 'But when he goes inside, how will we know which box the people are in? If we open the wrong one first the eyes'll look at us an' that's the finish of us!'

'We'll watch him tonight,' he decided, 'and maybe we'll find out his weakness – if he has one!'

After a while, Seán na Súl lumbered off into the fort. Fionn waited to see which window would light up. When he saw the flickering flame of a fire in the darkness he crept up to the window. Through a chink in the shutters he could see Seán stretched out on a bed of rushes while a turf fire blazed away in the hearth.

The two boxes were on top of each other just inside the door. The top box was slightly open so that the eyes could keep watch on the door all night to warn Seán na Súl of anyone coming in. At the first sign of movement they would begin to rattle loudly, enough to wake him, to do his worst to whoever was there.

Now Seán was settling down and soon he was snoring loudly. Fionn returned to his men. He said to Patrick, "Tis going to be no easy job to get past those eyes in their box.

'The only chance is to come up behind it, snap it down, and one of us keep our hands down on it while the others sweep the box with the people out of there. But how'll we manage that?'

'By Crom,' said Diarmaid, 'we'll have to think of something. We can't stay here all night just looking in at him sleeping.'

So they picked their way carefully into the dark, empty courtyard, ears cocked for any sound. But there was no sound, only the thin hiss of their own breathing and the thumping of their hearts. They stopped in the shadow of the battlements and Fionn whispered to Bran and Sceolan, 'I want you to go into his room and see what you can do. If you could even knock the box with the eyes in it down on the floor you'd be doing a great night's work. We'll do the rest.'

The dogs nodded and padded off down a gloomy passageway to the door of the room, Fionn and the men close behind. The door was unlocked. Seán na Súl felt so safe that he never locked a door at night. Fionn was fingering the bolt when Bran nosed ahead, pushing against the door with all his weight. The hinges creaked horribly and the eyes turned and rattled in their box, looking at the door. At the same moment Seán na Súl jumped up.

'Who's there?' he thundered, and sprang out of bed, snapped up the box with the eyes and made straight for the door.

Fionn held on to the bolt for dear life.

'I know you're there, whoever you are!' bellowed Seán na Súl, giving the door a savage drag.

'We'd better be off,' screeched Fionn. 'I can't hold the devil.'

The others stampeded back down the dark corridor while Fionn told Bran and Sceolan: 'Stay here, lads, and go for his legs when he comes out!'

Then he suddenly let go of the bolt, and at the same instant the ogre gave a violent pull – and landed on his back in the middle of the floor. The two dogs jumped on top of him, and then there was a confused din of battle, dogs snarling, Seán yowling and stamping, and the eyes rattling like mad things. Then there was a loud snap, and the rattling stopped at once.

'The box! it must have closed,' rapped Fionn. He ran back and peered into the room. The two dogs were at Seán na Súl's throat, Bran sitting on his chest. Fionn made a dash for the box.

'Patrick! Diarmaid! Quick!' he shouted. 'The other box, carry it out of here. Hurry!'

Patrick and Diarmaid clattered in, hoisted the box onto their shoulders and clomped out to the courtyard. At last, the two boxes were in their power. But the eyes were trying to break out of Fionn's box and he could hear the muffled rattling inside rising dangerously. He held on for his life, wrestling the lid to keep it closed. Only his mighty strength saved him: the eyes tired before he did.

Fionn stood there for a minute, catching his breath, then he went to the fireplace and flung the box into the flames The lid sprang open for the last time, the two eyes jumped out, into the fire, and a sudden shriek filled the room as if someone's face was being held in the flames. Then, WHIISSHHKK!! a blast of fire and smoke rushed up the chimney and at once Seán na Súl stopped struggling.

Before their eyes he began to change from the big rough man with a bandaged face to a young handsome lad with wavy curling hair and two eyes like any ordinary man.

He gaped up at them all.

'Where am I?' he asked, puzzled.

'*Who* are you?' exclaimed Fionn in a rough voice.

'Who are *you*?' replied the lad.

Fionn scratched his beard in amazement.

But he was not half as amazed as Patrick
and Diarmaid, who were out in the yard
listening to what was going on in the
room when their box snapped open and
people began to climb out of it. They
were climbing over each other, frantic,
every one of them, to get out into the
fresh air now that the spell was broken.

Patrick could only stand and watch, his mouth open. Never had he seen a miracle like this in all his travels.

One of the first to put his feet on the ground was a fine figure of a man, the chieftain of the fort himself. He strode over to Patrick and said, 'You must be the one who saved us from Seán na Súl.'

'Well, Fionn Mac Cumhail, the man that really saved you, is inside there in the room with that ugly fellow,' admitted Patrick.

'Draw every sword you have, men, and we'll face him this time. A reward for the first man to sweep the head off of him!'

They rushed down the corridor but the sight that greeted their eyes was not what they had expected. Before them stood Fionn and a handsome young man.

'Where's Seán na Súl?' cried the chief.

'Here he is,' answered Fionn quietly, 'this young man here. But let him explain it himself.'

The young man began:

'A good many years ago, my father, the prince of *Leacht Geal,* was having his dinner when this old woman came in looking for something to eat.

'Whatever ailed my father that day, he had the bad word for her.

'"Out of my dining-hall with you! We have no need of your likes here! I don't like the look of you," is what he said to her.

' "They're fine words, and fit for a prince, too,"
said she, mocking. "But from this day out you'll
have bitter cause to use the like, because your son
will be a changeling, a *malartán,* hee! hee! An' if you
don't like what you see now, he won't see anything
at all. You have my word for it!"

'With that, my father fell into a rage, a mighty
temper, and he called his guards to throw her out.

'We forgot all about it, but I was out hunting
in the forest one day about three years after when
who should I meet but the same woman. She stood
in the road in front of my horse and held up her
withered oul' hand.

' "Stop! You're the young prince, aren't you?"
she called out.

' "Move out of my way, dear woman," I said.
"Let me go my road."

‘ "You have no way only my way any more, boy," said she. "I know you well, and your father even better. I made you a promise years ago, a promise I'm going to keep this day."

‘With that, she pulled out a wand, touched my elbow, and I was changed into Seán na Súl.

‘ "A *malartán*, indeed," she cackled.

‘She made me wander the country, looking for people and bringing them back to her island to work for her. She said to me when she sent me out the first time, "The eyes you have in that box, they're mine, and they'll watch over you until your task for me is done. And that could take a good many lifetimes. Hee! Heeeee!"

'When you burned those eyes, Fionn, the spell
was broken and here I am now, safe and well.'

'An' I wonder what'll happen to herself?'
said Patrick.

If they only knew it, she was in a bad way.
For the rest of her days she was blind and wandered
the world, groping along by the walls crying in a
pitiful voice, 'Ohhh! Everything is dark. Where am
I going? Where am I going?'

And shortly after, hundreds of people began
to come ashore on the coast of Clare, wet and
bewildered, but safe. Among them were the children
of the old man of Ballyvaughan, and in a few days
they were reunited amid great rejoicing.

The young prince, as soon as he had rested and recovered from his frightening experiences, went home, and of course his father was delighted to see him.

'Where did you come from?' he cried. 'We thought you were dead.'

'That's a story to be told over a feast,' said the prince, 'but here are the men that saved me, Fionn Mac Cumhail, Diarmaid and Patrick.'

They bowed down to the prince of *Leacht Geal* – 'Good day, and good health to your lordship.'

'It is a great service you have done for me and mine,' said the prince. 'If there is any request you have, only say the word.'

Fionn and Diarmaid
would take nothing,
but Patrick asked if he
might have permission
to preach to the people
in the prince's lands
and convert them if he
could.

The prince gladly
gave it and Patrick had
soon converted all the
people of *Leacht Geal*
to the new religion.

Pronunciation guide

Cailleach – calyock (hag)

Ciaróg – keerogue (beetle)

Crom – crum

Diarmaid– dearmwid

Eamhain Macha – ow-wenn mocka

Fianna – feeanna

Fionn Mac Cumhail – finn mack cool

Hanam 'on diabhal – honnam on deeul (your soul to the devil)

Leacht Geal – lakht gyal

Malartán – mallartawn (changeling)

Oisín – usheen

Sceolan – shcole ann

Tír na nÓg – teer na nogue (land of eternal youth)

Tuath Clae – tooah clay